EIGHT-WHEEL
WONDER

BY JAKE MADDOX

text by
Shawn Pryor

STONE ARCH BOOKS
a capstone imprint

Published by Stone Arch Books, an imprint of Capstone.
1710 Roe Crest Drive, North Mankato, Minnesota 56003
capstonepub.com

Library of Congress Cataloging-in-Publication Data is available on the Library of Congress website.
ISBN: 9781666344868 (hardcover)
ISBN: 9781666344905 (paperback)
ISBN: 9781666344912 (ebook PDF)

Summary: Kadijah Carrie—aka KC—is obsessed with roller skating. When its revival goes viral on the internet, she shows her parents and friends all the cool videos and tricks she can find. Then Kadijah discovers the world of roller speed skating, and she is determined to take part in a local speed skating tournament. But there's a tiny problem . . . Kadijah doesn't know how to skate. Will the help of her friends and a stint at a fast-food drive-in get Kadijah up to speed for the race, or will she wipe out?

Editorial Credits
Designer: Tracy Davies; Media Researcher: Svetlana Zhurkin;
Production Specialist: Katy LaVigne

Image Credits
Shutterstock: Brocreative, 2–3 and throughout, Dmitry Morgan, cover, 1, and throughout, goffkein.pro, back cover and throughout, Isniper, 86–87, 88–89

Printed and bound in the USA. 4882

TABLE OF CONTENTS

CHAPTER I

OBSESSED

In the cafeteria at Fairbright Middle School, thirteen-year-old Kadijah Carrie sat with her friends Damon and Zoey, eating lunch.

"I've been dying to show you all this skate dancing tricks video I saw on ZooTube!" said Kadijah as she pulled out her phone.

Damon munched on his pizza. "Did you all see the SkateTokk video links I sent last night?"

The three of them had been watching skate dancing videos ever since they'd seen some people doing skate tricks at the park a couple of weeks ago.

Seeing the skaters had made Kadijah want to get out her old roller skates and give them a try, but she hadn't used them in years. Besides, she was sure they would be too small by now.

"I did! The group dancing one with the Harlem Shake was so cool!" said Zoey. "I wish I could dance on skates like they do. But since I don't like falling, I'll stick with regular dancing."

Kadijah and Damon laughed. "Trust me, I feel the same way," said Kadijah. "But maybe it would be good for us to try something new."

"Maybe," said Zoey as she and Damon huddled closer to Kadijah. "Let's see this video!"

Kadijah pressed play on her phone as the trio watched. A group of hip-hop skaters did some break dancing moves, then transitioned into a mix of ballet-meets-break dancing moves, followed by flips and slow-motion moonwalks.

The three friends watched the video in awe. Their mouths were wide open as the video ended.

"Did you see those moves? The way that one guy did a moonwalk and then flipped into a one-arm handstand? Is that for real? WOW!" said Damon.

Zoey rubbed her chin. "How did that skater do a backflip off of a brick wall with skates on? Just . . . how?"

"I thought you'd like that," said Kadijah. She picked up her fork as another video began playing automatically.

"Eight-hundred meter speed skaters, prepare to race!" said an announcer on the video as a group of six teens lined up on an oval-shaped rink.

Kadijah couldn't take her eyes off the screen.

"On your mark, get set . . . " said the announcer. "Go!" A buzzer sounded, and the skaters took off like arrows.

"Hey KC, are you going to eat your pizza?" asked Zoey.

Kadijah ignored her, all her attention on the video.

"KC, are you with us?"

7

"The speed skaters are making their turn," said Kadijah as she pushed her lunch tray toward Zoey. "Take my slice but leave the salad and brownie for me. I'm watching this race!"

"Race?" said Damon. He leaned in. Zoey was busy digging into Kadijah's pepperoni pizza.

"It's like running track, but instead of running, they're on skates!" said Kadijah. "It's the last lap, and three of the skaters are neck and neck for first place. It's going to be a close one!"

"Look at those skates!" Zoey said, leaning in to watch too. "They aren't like the skates the trick skaters use. Their wheels are in a row instead of side by side."

Damon chimed in. "They're inline skates. They're built for speed. My cousin has some."

"Shhh—the race is almost over!" Kadijah said. "It's down to two skaters for first place. Look at how fast they're going! The racer with the blue helmet is leaning forward to reach for the win—yes!"

Kadijah smiled as the video ended. "What a rush,

and I wasn't even part of the race! Inline speed racing looks *so* cool!" Before she could say more, a video ad played.

"Fairbright, get ready for the Speed Skating Tournament one month from now! We'll have racing events for all levels and ages! Lots of prizes! Winners in the tourney will qualify for the state tournament later this year! Don't delay, sign up today!" boomed the voice-over in the ad.

"Speed skating in our town? Cool!" said Damon. "I wonder if my cousin will be in it . . ."

Zoey licked the last bit of pizza sauce off her fingers. "I'm down to go watch if you all are. What do you think, KC?"

Kadijah was still staring down at her phone.

"KC?" said Damon.

Kadijah snapped out of her trance. "Huh? Yeah, yeah, I want to go, for sure!"

But I think I want to do more than just watch, Kadijah thought. *I want to race.*

***

After school, the trio of Kadijah, Damon, and
Zoey walked home. Kadijah was fixated on her
phone, replaying the speed skating race again and
again.

"That's the zillionth time you've watched that
video today, KC. You're obsessed," said Zoey.

Damon added, "She almost got her phone taken
away in math class because she was watching it while
class was starting."

Kadijah finally put her phone away. "Sorry. I just
think this speed skating stuff is so cool."

"Well, in a couple of weeks we'll get to go see it
live," said Damon.

"I want to do more than just *watch* it," said
Kadijah.

Zoey and Damon turned to look at her. "What do
you mean?" they said in unison.

Kadijah smiled. "I mean . . . I want to compete!"

Her friends had unsure looks on their faces.

"But you've never even speed skated before," said Zoey. "And when was the last time you skated at all? Like, third grade?"

"KC, the race is only a month from now," said Damon. "It's going to take a lot of training to be able to get out there and compete with kids our age who have been racing for years."

"It can't be that hard," Kadijah said. "All I need is some inline skates. I already know how to go fast with regular skates, or at least I used to. Just imagine how much faster I'll be with the right gear!"

Zoey shook her head. "I don't think it's going to be that easy, but if you want to do it, then go for it. You definitely need inline skates, though."

"And you need someone to help you train," said Damon. "We don't know anything about speed skating . . . like, at all."

Kadijah smiled. "I'll check ZooTube for training videos. I spent all my birthday money on video games, but maybe my parents will buy me a pair of inline skates."

Zoey pulled out her phone and started searching. "Well, I'm looking at prices for inline skates, and a good pair for competition and racing starts at around two hundred dollars. Just how generous are your parents?"

"Maybe I can ask them and promise to pay them back after I make the state tournament," Kadijah said confidently.

"State tournament? You haven't even signed up for the local tourney yet!" Damon said.

"You know the one thing that KC never lacks is confidence," Zoey said with a laugh.

Kadijah gave Zoey a playful shove. "Yeah, I'm not hiding under any rock. You gotta believe in yourself!"

"It's going to take more than believing. You're going to have to *work* for this if you want to have any sort of chance," said Zoey. "Of course we'll be rooting for you, though. We support you—always."

"Absolutely," said Damon. "But . . . you've never played in any organized sport, KC. It may be tougher than you think."

Kadijah wasn't concerned. "You two worry too much. I'm going to get the skates, start training, and knock out the competition at the tournament next month. *Boom, boom, boom*. Just wait and see!"

"Okay, can we stop talking about speed skating? We're near Carl's Ice Cream Shoppe. Let's get something sweet!" said Zoey.

"Race you there! Loser has to buy ice cream for everyone else!" said Damon as he took off running.

Kadijah and Zoey took off after him. "You got a head start, cheater!" shouted Kadijah.

CHAPTER 2

THERE'S A PROBLEM . . .

Kadijah made her double scoop of strawberry banana delight last for the entire walk home. She dropped her backpack by the front door, kicked off her shoes, and slid across the wood floor into the living room.

"Hey kiddo, how was school today?" Dad asked.

"School was fine. No homework, so that's a win," said Kadijah. "But I've got some news!"

"What is it?" asked Mom.

Full of excitement, Kadijah exclaimed, "I'm going to sign up for the speed skating tournament!"

Her parents were confused. "Speed skating? Tournament?" asked Dad.

"But . . . you don't speed skate?" Mom's statement sounded more like a question.

"Yeah, but it's a whole month away. I can learn," Kadijah said.

She showed her parents the tournament website on her phone. "And when I win in my age bracket, I'll automatically qualify for the state tournament! I saw a speed skating video today, and I've just got to do this!" she said.

Kadijah's dad took off his glasses and rubbed his forehead. "Today. You decided this all today? Kadijah, there have been plenty of times that you wanted to do something only to quit when things became too hard or didn't go your way."

"Remember when you quit during basketball tryouts?" Mom offered helpfully.

Kadijah frowned. "I didn't know they'd be throwing so many elbows," Kadijah said. "That hurt!"

"Or how about when you wanted to play soccer and quit after the first game?" said Dad.

"The ball hit me in the face and left a knot on my forehead for a week!" said Kadijah.

"And remember when we paid for all that equipment for softball? After three games you—"

"Okay, okay, okay. I get it. You've been keeping score on my fails. Sure, I get excited about things, and sometimes I do quit. But this time is different. I used to love roller skating as a kid. And I should be able to pick up on speed skating without any problems. I really, really want to do this," Kadijah said.

Mom put her hand on Kadijah's shoulder. "Honey, if you're actually serious about this, we'll help you with it. But you've got to show some commitment."

"I will, Mom!" Kadijah said.

"And how much do these inline skates cost?" asked Dad.

Kadijah took back her phone, pulled up a website, and handed the phone to him. "Jake's Sporting Goods and Yogurt Shop in town sells them."

"Two hundred dollars?" Dad hollered and then clutched his chest dramatically. "That's expensive!"

"Well, they do buy used sports equipment there," said Mom. "How about if we take all the equipment that Kadijah quit using—or never used—and trade it in? With the store credit and her chore allowance, she can get inline skates and pay her entrance fee to the tourney."

Kadijah started jumping up and down in delight. "Yes! Great idea, Mom! See, you guys won't have to spend any money at all, and I get to be a speed skater! Win win! I promise that I won't quit! Please, Dad? Please??????"

"Well . . . all right then," said Dad, "We'll go to the store tomorrow."

Kadijah took off down the hall, sliding toward her room. "I'm going to get all my old sports gear together right now, and then I'm going to tell Damon and Zoey! This is going to be great! Thank you so much, Mom and Dad!"

***

A couple of days later, Kadijah met her friends at the park. She was sitting on a bench with her skate helmet, kneepads, and arm pads on.

"Hey KC!" Zoey and Damon called out as they rolled up to Kadijah on their bikes.

"Hey guys!" said Kadijah. She had just taken off her sneakers and was opening up a large shoebox.

"Did you get your inline skates?" asked Damon.

"I sure did," said Kadijah. "After I traded in my old sports equipment, I had over two hundred and fifty dollars in trade and upgraded to a high-end pair of speed skates!" She opened the shoebox to reveal a pair of gold and black inline skates with shiny gold wheels.

"Look at these beauties!" she said proudly.

"WOW!" said Zoey.

"So, you've got the skates. Now, are you ready to train?" asked Damon.

"Of course!" Kadijah said as she put on the skates and laced them up. "I watched a bunch of videos today, and I'm ready to show you all how fast I am!"

After cinching up a double knot, she stood up and immediately started to wobble. "I can't keep my balance!" she screamed as she fell to the ground with a *thud*.

She lay flat on her back, looking up at her friends. "Let's try that again," she said after taking a beat.

Trying to get back on her feet, she wobbled and flopped around like one of those inflatable puppets at car dealers.

"Why is it so hard to stand up? They're just skates!" complained Kadijah.

"Well, it's been a long time. And you were like a foot shorter last time you did this. Maybe your center of gravity has changed?" Zoey suggested.

Damon and Zoey each took one of Kadijah's hands, pulled her up, then held her steady.

"How about if we hold on to you and run alongside you for awhile until you get used to your new skates?" suggested Zoey.

But before Kadijah could answer, she started to lose her balance and fell again, this time taking Zoey's bike down with her.

Kadijah sighed. The thought of quitting crept into her mind, but she shut it down immediately.

I can do this! she told herself. *Maybe . . .*

CHAPTER 3

FAST FOOD TO THE RESCUE!

A few days later, Kadijah, Damon, and Zoey were at The Burger Break diner after school, sharing a basket of french fries. Damon and Zoey were very cheerful, but Kadijah was mopey.

"You've been so quiet at school," Damon said. "Mr. Daniels hasn't even had to tell you to stop watching ZooTube videos in math class lately. What's up?"

"I don't know," Kadijah said with a sigh.

"You haven't been responding to our texts. We were lucky to get you to come out with us," Zoey said. "Look, we know the skate training isn't going great . . ."

23

Kadijah huffed. "It isn't going *at all*. I'm scared to try again. Even the basic training videos I've watched are too advanced for me. You were right. My parents were right. I should just quit like I always do, before I make a bigger fool of myself."

"Well, that attitude isn't going to get you anywhere," said Damon. "How bad do you want this, KC?"

"Really, really bad, Damon," Kadijah said. "But if I can't even stay upright, then how am I supposed to race? I don't want to embarrass myself in front of everybody at the tournament!"

Kadijah let out a loud sigh, then looked at Zoey. However, Zoey wasn't paying attention to the conversation anymore. Her eyes were focused on something else.

On someone else.

"What are you looking at, Zoey?" asked Kadijah.

It was an older teen working at The Burger Break, zipping around on inline skates, taking customers' orders and dropping off food with the grace of a dancer and the speed of a racer.

"WOW," Kadijah said. "That's awesome! It doesn't even look like she's trying. It's like she's skating on air!"

Damon looked over. "*That's* my cousin Trini!" he exclaimed. "I didn't know she worked here now. Maybe you should ask her to help you train for the tournament."

"It's fate!" Zoey declared. "Even if she doesn't know about speed skating, she could at least teach you the basics so you can stand up in those expensive skates for more than five seconds."

"I don't know," Kadijah said. "I'm sure she's super busy and doesn't want to be bothered with a kid. Like—wait, what are you two *doing?*"

Kadijah panicked as Zoey and Damon waved their arms excitedly, trying to get Trini's attention.

"We're getting you some training, that's what we're doing," said Zoey.

"Here she comes!" said Damon.

Kadijah gulped nervously. *What if she says no?*
What if she laughs at me when I tell her that I can't use my
inline skates? I'll be so embarrassed.

Trini rolled up beside their table. "Damon! What
are you doing here?" She gave him a high five. "Who
are your friends?"

Zoey took over the conversation before Damon
could respond. "Hi Trini. I'm Zoey and that's
Kadijah—or KC. We saw your skating skills. You're
incredible! How long have you been using inline
skates?"

"Oh, thanks," Trini replied. "I've been zooming
on inlines for years. I'm also a speed skater, so I wear
my skates during my shifts to work on my agility and
focus."

"Did you hear that, KC?" said Zoey as she stared
pointedly at her friend. "What a *coincidence!* Aren't you
going to be in a tournament here in Fairbright next
month?"

Kadijah's face was flushed with humiliation. She gritted her teeth as she said, "Yes, Zoey, that's the plan."

"That's awesome—I'll be competing too!" Trini said to Kadijah. "How long have you been speed skating?"

Kadijah let out a big sigh. "Well, the problem is that I've never technically speed skated before. I thought it would be easy to learn. I got a nice pair of inline skates, but I can barely stand up in them. The race is next month, and I don't know what to do. I'm kind of a mess. Do you have any tips for me?"

Behind Kadijah's back, Damon smiled at Trini and put his hands together to plead with his cousin.

Trini paused as she saw Kadijah's head begin to tilt down in defeat. "I'll tell you what. If you're serious about wanting to do this, meet me at the park tomorrow. Let's see if we can get you upright and going."

"You'll train me?" Kadijah smiled.

"I will, but you have to be willing to listen to me and do what I say. If you put the work in, I'll have you speed skating in no time," said Trini.

Damon mouthed "thank you" to his cousin, while Kadijah beamed up at her.

"You're the best!" Kadijah squealed.

CHAPTER 4

CRAWL BEFORE YOU CAN WALK

The next day, Kadijah met Trini at the park as planned.

"Hey, Trini! Thanks again for helping me train," Kadijah said. "I really appreciate it."

"I hope you're ready to work today," Trini replied. "We've got a lot to do. Do you want me to call you Kadijah or KC?"

"KC's fine—all my friends call me that."

Trini nodded and smiled. "KC it is."

"Should I try to put my inline skates on so I can learn to stand up in them?" asked Kadijah.

29

Trini shook her head. "We're not going to worry about putting on skates today."

Kadijah was confused. "But how am I supposed to learn about speed skating if I don't put on my skates?"

Trini smiled. "If you're struggling to stand up in those skates, then that means that we need to work on your core strength first."

"Core what?" Kadijah asked. She was picturing an apple.

Trini pointed to her stomach. "Your stomach is the core that helps you balance," she explained. "If you strengthen your core, it will help you stay steady on the skates. We'll work on your ankle strength too. You can't skate without that."

She walked Kadijah over to a set of exercise equipment and pointed toward a wooden disk that had springs underneath it.

"Hop up on that balance board. We're going to see how well you can balance yourself," Trini said.

"Here goes nothing," Kadijah said. She put one

foot on the balance board, then the other. The board began to shake. "It's really wobbly!"

"It's you who's wobbly—not the board!" Trini joked. "Keep your feet hip-distance apart, near the edges of the board."

The front of the balance board hit the ground, forcing Kadijah to hop off it and onto the ground. "At least this time I didn't fall on my face," she said, relieved to have landed on her feet.

"Maybe I should show you how to get *on* a balance board," said Trini.

She stepped onto the middle of the board, shifted her feet so that they were close to the edges, and placed her arms out in front of her.

"When you get on the board, the goal is to keep your posture straight, keep your feet apart, and shift your weight so that the edges of the board never touch the ground until you get off," Trini explained as she balanced easily on the board.

Kadijah was impressed. "Wow, you've been on

the board for over a minute straight!"

Trini hopped off. "With practice, you'll be able to do the same. Hop back on and let's see how long you can stay on. Once you get good at standing on it, we'll get you doing squats and side-to-side exercises on it."

"Let's do it!" said Kadijah.

* * *

After some time on the balance board and doing other exercises, Trini handed Kadijah a pair of regular roller skates. "Here, put these on."

Kadijah took the skates from Trini and gave them a disappointed look. "Why do I need to put old roller skates on? I can't speed skate in these."

"You're not ready to put on the inline skates just yet. Also, have you ever skated fast in regular roller skates?" asked Trini.

"Um, define fast," said Kadijah sheepishly.

Trini laughed. "Okay, let's just try it out for a bit and see how it goes."

They skated around the paved areas of the park. Within a few minutes, Kadijah began to remember the feel of skating, and her confidence grew. The skates started to feel comfortable, like they were more an extension of her and not two slippery jellyfish strapped to her feet. She watched every move Trini made and tried to imitate her.

"How's it feel?" Trini asked after a while.

"I feel pretty good! I haven't thought once about falling or tripping. But I noticed that sometimes you stop not with your brake, but by doing some funky thing with your legs. What's that move called?" Kadijah asked.

"Great question. It's called a plow stop or v-stop. That's when I spread my legs out wider than the width of my shoulders, and I turn my toes toward each other to slow down or stop," Trini replied.

Kadijah nodded while she copied the move.

"But remember to brace yourself and try to keep your core balanced when you do a plow stop, or else your momentum as you slow down will cause you to fall forward," warned Trini.

Kadijah nodded and patted her belly. "Core power!" she said.

"So now we're going to pick up the pace with speed intervals," Trini went on. "Since you're more familiar with regular skates, you should feel steadier than on the inlines. For a bit we'll skate at a regular pace, then we're going to take off as fast as we can, and then we'll slow down again."

Kadijah nodded. "I'll try my best to keep up!"

"Speed intervals will help you with your overall stamina. Stamina is one of the keys in speed skating," Trini said.

"Stamina. Got it," Kadijah said, eager to be a good student.

"Okay, let's go!" said Trini.

The pair took off side by side on the paved park

trail. For a couple of minutes they skated at a leisurely pace.

"Now, take off!" yelled Trini. She launched into a sprint, catching Kadijah off guard.

Wow, she's really fast. I'm going to have to get focused if I want to keep up with her, Kadijah thought.

She dug her toes in and worked to catch up with Trini.

"You've got some wheels—you caught up with me pretty fast!" said Trini as they began to slow down again. "And that's on those old skates!"

Kadijah was panting but smiling. "Just wait until I'm able to put on my inline skates. I'm going to blaze past everybody!"

Trini laughed. "I admire your confidence. Okay, get ready to take off again . . . . Go!"

CHAPTER 5

NEW SKILLS

After school, Kadijah ran to her locker. *Today's the day I finally get to inline skate with Trini!*

Kadijah had been doing the exercises Trini had showed her—sit-ups, toe ups, ankle rolls . . . all to help with core and ankle strength. Kadijah was amazed at how much stronger she seemed after just a week. She felt ready to tie on her inline skates and blast off like a rocket.

"Hey, KC!" said Damon, as he and Zoey approached Kadijah's locker. "We're going to study at the library. You want to come?"

"Can't make it. I have more training with Trini today. We're meeting at The Burger Break," Kadijah said.

"We've barely hung out all week. You must be working really hard!" Zoey said, impressed.

Kadijah smiled. "You know it! Trini has helped me work on my strength, balance, speed, and proper breathing. I feel great! And now that I've got all that stuff solved, I'm ready to smoke the competition!"

"But have you actually been on the new skates yet?" Damon asked.

"Don't question the process!" Kadijah shot back.

"Well, we'll hang out later this week if you have the time. Don't want to make you late. Coach Trini can be hard core," Damon joked.

"Good luck! Text us after you're done and let us know how it went!" called Zoey as the flow of students swallowed the two of them up.

Kadijah closed her locker and headed toward the exit, ready to race.

Kadijah looked around The Burger Break for Trini.

Where is she? I know I'm not late . . .

Suddenly, Trini rolled up behind her, wearing her inline skates and Burger Break uniform. "Hey KC, you ready?"

Kadijah was confused. "Why are you in your work uniform? I thought we were working out today."

Trini smiled and handed Kadijah a Burger Break T-shirt. "We are. I talked to my boss, and she's going to let you shadow me at work for a few hours today."

"Hey, I'm happy to help—and maybe score some free fries—but how will following you help me with speed skating?" Kadijah asked.

"It's about agility—knowing when to speed up, predicting when to slow down, and everything in between. It will also help you break in those inline skates. And the best way to do that, now that you've got your balance, is the wait staff challenge," Trini said with a smile.

Kadijah started to look around the restaurant. It was full of tables, chairs, and customers getting up and down and moving around.

"It's like an obstacle course!" Kadijah said, a bit overwhelmed.

Trini laughed. "Exactly! Just stay next to me and do what I do, okay?"

"You got it, boss," Kadijah said. She pulled on the Burger Break tee over her tank and saluted Trini. "KC, reporting for duty!"

***

"Order up for table twelve!" shouted the cook as he put plates of food on a tray and clanged a bell.

Pop songs from the 1950s played from the speakers, and Trini bopped to the music as she zipped between tables and chairs, taking orders, delivering food, and refilling drinks.

Wearing her inline skates, Kadijah did her best to keep up with her. But it wasn't as effortless as Trini made it look.

"Order up for table fifteen!" the cook shouted.

Trini skated over to the counter and picked up the tray. Then she handed it to Kadijah.

"Your turn! Are you ready to take this tray to our customers?" Trini asked.

Kadijah's eyes got big. "You want me to take the tray? But what if I fall, or spill the food on somebody, or—"

"You're going to do just fine, and I'll be right behind you," said Trini as she handed her the tray of food. "It's just two burgers and fries. You got this."

Kadijah took a deep breath. She gripped the tray and headed off for table fifteen. "Okay. Here we go!"

As she skated across the floor, table fifteen seemed miles away.

"You got this, you got this," Kadijah mumbled under her breath, giving herself a pep talk as she went. But then, from out of nowhere, a little girl came running right at her.

"Look out!" Kadijah yelled and spun out of the child's way. "Phew, that was a close—"

Before she could finish her sentence, a customer pushed his chair out, bumping into Kadijah.

"Whoa-whoa-whoa! Heads up!" said Kadijah as she started to flail. But she maintained her balance and kept the food from slipping off the tray.

"Sorry!" yelled the customer.

Finally, Kadijah was approaching table fifteen. She decided to try the plow stop. But as she started to spread her legs, she failed to take into consideration the weight of the tray, which threw off her balance. The food on the tray started to slide forward. *Uh-oh!* she thought.

Watching Kadijah and sensing her panic, the mother at table fifteen threw her arms over her kid to protect him from the impending disaster.

But at the last moment, Kadijah regained her balance and control of the tray. She came to a perfect stop at the table.

"Here's your order! One Big Break burger, a Baby Break burger, and a basket of fries. Do you need anything else?" Kadijah said casually, as if she'd never lost control.

"Nope, we're good. Thank you!" said the mother.

"That was awesome!" yelled the little boy.

"Thanks. Enjoy your meal!" said Kadijah. She turned around, expecting to see Trini right behind her. "Did you see how awesome—"

But Trini wasn't there at all. She was back at the counter, smiling. And clapping. Kadijah skated back to her.

"Hey, you tricked me! You said you'd be right behind me!" Kadijah exclaimed.

"Sometimes a teacher has to let a student go on their own to see if they're making progress. And after that order delivery, I'd say you're doing great!" Trini said, giving Kadijah a high five.

"Thanks! Does this mean I get a promotion?" Kadijah joked.

"I wouldn't go that far," laughed Trini. "But you've made a great leap today."

Kadijah was proud of herself. *I'm doing it. I'm actually learning how to use these skates! And soon Trini will teach me how to race on a speed skating track. It feels so good to know that I can actually do this!*

"Order up for table twenty-six!" shouted the cook as he put the plates of food on two trays and rang the bell. Trini handed Kadijah one tray and then took the other.

"Right this way!" Kadijah said and took off for table twenty-six.

"I'll see if I can keep up with you!" Trini replied, laughing.

***

After training was over for the day, Kadijah's parents picked her up. She hopped in the car and waved to Trini as they pulled away.

"How did training go, KC?" Dad asked.

"It was so awesome!" Kadijah said. "Trini says I'm agile! I'm able to keep my balance better now. Trini is such a great teacher."

In the front seat, Mom smiled. "We're so proud of you and all of your hard work, honey."

"Thanks, Mom," Kadijah replied.

Mom turned in her seat. "Have a look in that bag. Dad and I got you a surprise."

Kadijah looked at the large shopping bag on the back seat next to her. She peeked inside it and began pulling out items.

"Wow! Look at all this cool speed skating gear! A spandex suit, new helmet, skating gloves, knee and shin pads—this is everything else I needed before the tournament! Thank you!" Kadijah squealed.

"It's just our way of saying that we believe in you, KC. You've got this," Dad replied.

Kadijah smiled. It felt so good to hear that, and it made her believe in herself even more.

CHAPTER 6

TRIAL RUN

Within a few days, it was time for speed sessions at the roller track.

Kadijah and her friends met up at the track. Damon had brought a little sign that read "Kick It KC!"

"Are you excited about today?" Zoey asked.

"Definitely," said Kadijah as she put on her skates and safety gear. "All my training with Trini has led up to this point."

"Can't wait to see you get out there!" said Damon.

In a moment, Trini arrived. She smiled and reached out to fist-bump Kadijah.

"You ready to hit the track, KC?" she asked.

"Let's go!" Kadijah said.

The two of them skated onto the track while Zoey and Damon cheered from the sidelines.

"Hmm, skating on this track feels different than the paved park trails and the Burger Break floors," Kadijah said. "What kind of track is this?"

"A speed skating track is usually a hundred-meter circle on plastic-coated wood floors or concrete," Trini explained. "A race can be up to twenty-five or more laps. Your race will be four hundred meters, or four laps. Come on, let's take a few warm-up laps so you can get a feel for it."

Kadijah noticed that the track curved upward at the edges.

I need to be careful on the turns and control my speed and balance when we start going full speed. I don't want to fly off at the turns!

"When we skate during a race, the key is to bend your upper body forward, and try to be as small as possible. Doing that reduces your air friction," said Trini.

"I get it. The more compact I am, the faster I can go!" Kadijah said.

Kadijah enjoyed the feel of gliding along the track. In the ZooTube videos, she had fallen in love with that magical, flying sensation that the skaters seemed to experience, and now she was feeling it too. It was like nothing she'd ever done before.

"What do you think?" asked Trini as they completed their fourth lap and slowed to a stop in front of Damon and Zoey. They were sitting in the stands eating popcorn like they were at a pro sporting event.

"It's amazing! I can go faster on this type of track, for sure," Kadijah replied.

"Speed skating isn't just about going fast," said Trini. "It's also about learning how to pace yourself and knowing when to use the skater in front of you to your advantage."

"How would you do that?" Zoey asked.

"Watch us. I'm going to go fast, and KC will catch up to me and stay as close as she can behind me. It's called drafting," said Trini.

"I know what that is!" said Damon. "They do that in car races!"

"Exactly!" Trini said. "Drafting can help you save energy when you skate. If you're behind someone, you have less wind resistance going against you."

"The skater in front is blocking more wind, so I don't have to use as much effort. Then, when the moment is right, I can kick into high gear and pass!" Kadijah said triumphantly. "I may have watched some speed skating videos before coming out here today," she admitted.

"Well, you got it right!" Trini replied. "Drafting saves up some power so you have something left for the final sprint."

Kadijah tightened the strap on her helmet. "I'm ready, Trini."

Trini quickly took off, and Kadijah skated as fast as she could to catch up to her. As they got to the first turn, Kadijah was right behind Trini.

Wow, there's less wind pushing back on me when I'm drafting behind her, Kadijah thought. *This is awesome!*

"As we're rounding the next curve, turn on your rockets and zoom past me!" yelled Trini.

As they hit the turn, Kadijah pushed as fast and hard as she could. Exerting all her effort, Kadijah inched past Trini!

Zoey and Damon cheered. "She did it! Just like the race car drivers do!" Damon yelled.

"Way to go, KC!" said Zoey as Kadijah and Trini came to a stop in front of them again.

Kadijah was so happy. "How did I do, coach?"

Trini smiled at Kadijah. "You did pretty good," she said. "Let's keep practicing your drafting and your takeoffs at the starting line today. Then tomorrow, I'll have a special surprise for you."

"A surprise?" Kadijah said.

She was already having so much fun, she couldn't imagine how it could get any better.

Zoey pulled out her phone. "I'm going to record you so you can show your mom and dad how great you're doing at this!"

"Ready for another round?" asked Trini.

"So ready," Kadijah replied.

"Go!" Trini replied.

***

The next day at the track, Kadijah and her friends waited for Trini to arrive.

"I wonder what Trini's surprise will be?" asked Zoey.

"Whatever the surprise is, I'm ready. The preliminaries for the tournament are next week, and I can't wait to show everyone what I can do!" Kadijah said confidently. "Hey, there's Trini!"

"It looks like she's brought some friends with her,"

said Zoey as Trini and three others walked up to them.

"Hey guys, these are my friends Corey, Stacy, and Ivy," said Trini. "They're speed skaters too. This is KC, Zoey, and my baby cousin, Damon," she teased.

Damon made a face at Trini, and Trini and her friends laughed.

"Nice to meet you all," said Kadijah. "So Trini, what's the surprise?"

"The surprise is we're going to have a trial race, and you're going to race against me and my friends. It'll be just like a real race, cuz none of us are going to hold back," Trini said.

Stacy chimed in. "Practicing with older kids will give you the advantage for your race next week with your age group."

"What are we waiting for? Let's line up and race!" Kadijah said, rolling back and forth on her skates as if revving her engine.

"First race is going to be four hundred meters, or four laps around the track," Trini said as the racers gathered at the starting line.

"Count us down, Zoey!" Trini said.

"On your mark, get set . . . go!" screamed Zoey, and the skaters took off.

Kadijah sped up as quickly as she could. The group was bunched together at first but then began to spread apart. Halfway through the first lap, Kadijah was in last place, trailing Stacy.

Remember what Trini taught you. Stay low, lean forward, and draft to conserve your energy. Then kick into high gear and pass!

Kadijah settled into her position and stride as she caught up to Stacy and tucked in behind her to draft.

Okay . . . we're coming up on the turn . . . ready . . . punch it!

Kadijah kicked into high gear and passed Stacy to move into fourth place. Three laps to go.

The other racers were very fast, and Stacy was on

her tail, but Kadijah was determined to move up in the ranks.

In the next lap, she passed Corey and moved into third place. In the final lap, Kadijah came close to overtaking Ivy for second place, but Ivy pushed into another gear.

Kadijah watched hopelessly as Ivy and Trini crossed the finish line ahead of her.

But her disappointment didn't last long. *She had finished third! In her first practice race!*

Kadijah was exhausted but elated.

The racers all high-fived each other.

"You blew me away, KC!" Stacy said, bending over and pressing on a stitch in her side.

Zoey and Damon ran over to the racers and handed them bottles of water.

"KC, you did great out there!" said Zoey. "Wait till you see the videos I took. You're gonna be amazed!"

"You're getting really good at drafting!" added Damon. "I'm gonna call you Stealth Lightning!" he said and made an electric *zappp* sound.

Trini looked at Kadijah. "You just raced against four very experienced high schoolers who have been speed skating for years. We're older than you and we're fast, and you *still* passed Stacy and Corey!"

"I could only wish I was that fast when I was your age!" said Corey.

"And you almost caught up to me! Just wait until you compete against kids your own age. You're going to kill it out there!" said Ivy.

"Really?" said Kadijah.

"Yes, really," Trini said. "This was your first ever race. And the more you race, the better you'll be."

Kadijah smiled. "Can we go again?"

Stacy smiled. "You thought we were only going to race one time? I'm not going to leave here till I place higher than you today!"

Trini laughed. "All right, let's take our water break and stretch a bit. Next race, we'll pull out *all* the stops."

"You're on!" said Kadijah.

Zoey and Damon made more zapping lightning sounds from the stands.

Kadijah shouted, "Get ready for a storm!"

CHAPTER 7

WIPEOUT!

The day of the Fairbright Speed Skating Tournament had finally arrived. Kadijah, her family, and her friends were all at the skate track that morning. The stands were packed with fans.

"You ready for your big race today, Lightning?" asked Dad. He had heard about Damon's new nickname for Kadijah.

Kadijah smiled. "I was born ready!" she replied and shook her fist in the air triumphantly.

"Can you believe how many skaters are here?

There are so many kids in my division that our races had to be split up between this weekend and next weekend!" Kadijah said.

"I had no idea it would be THIS big," Mom said. "This is so exciting!"

Just then, Trini walked up to Kadijah and the others. "Hey, everybody!"

"Hi, Trini!" Kadijah replied. "Did you come to see me race? It starts in a half hour!"

"Of course! My race doesn't start till later this afternoon, so my friends and I will be in the stands rooting for you," Trini said as she pointed over to Stacy, Corey, and Ivy.

"We saved some extra seats if you want to join us!" she said to Kadijah's parents.

"That's so nice of you," said Mom. "And thank you for being such a great help to Kadijah. She has nothing but wonderful things to say about you."

"You're welcome," Trini said. "KC's very talented, and if she keeps at it, there's a really good chance that she could go far in speed skating."

"Let's go get those seats. Good luck, kiddo!" said Dad.

Damon waved his "Kick It KC!" sign and said, "Break a leg, Stealth Lightning!"

"I think that's only for theater, Damon," said Zoey. "What he meant was, knock 'em dead!"

"No matter what happens, we're proud of you!" said Mom. She gave Kadijah a quick hug before they headed off to their seats.

Kadijah smiled and gave them a big thumbs-up. Then she went to prepare for her race.

***

"Middle school girls heat six, get ready for the four-hundred meter race!" the announcer said over the speaker system.

Kadijah and four other girls rolled up to the starting line. Kadijah sized up her competition. A tall lanky girl named Leesha, a short muscular girl named Annie, and two average size girls, like Kadijah, lined up beside her. She wasn't going to rule any of them out. Any one of them could have more experience or more stamina than she had.

But Kadijah knew one thing for certain—none of them had more determination than she did.

I'll blast out of the gate before they even know what hit them, Kadijah thought, psyching herself up.

"When the pistol fires, begin! Good luck!" said the announcer. "On your mark!"

The girls bent and leaned forward, ready to race.

I'm going to get first place and move on to the next round. Then I'll advance to the state tournament . . .

"Get set . . . "

Get ready to eat my dust!

Bang! The starter pistol fired, and the racers took off. By the first turn, Kadijah already had a sizable lead on her competition.

"Go, Kadijah, go!" Kadijah heard her mom cheer.

"Pace yourself, KC! You got this!" yelled Trini.

For the first lap, Kadijah held on to the lead, but in the second lap, Annie pulled ahead.

That's okay, Kadijah thought. *I'll draft behind her for a while, regain my strength, and then I'll blaze past her!*

"Good job, KC! Nice drafting!" yelled Damon.

By the time the skaters started the third lap, Kadijah was still drafting close behind Annie. But the other skaters were catching up. Soon all five skaters were bunched together as they raced. Kadijah was feeling crowded.

That's okay, she thought. *When we hit the fourth turn on this lap, I'll zoom past the leader and kick it into overdrive for the final lap and an easy win! I beat two high schoolers already—I can definitely beat these middle schoolers.*

The speed skaters were still clustered close to

each other in the third lap, going at full speed as they headed into the turn.

It's time for overdrive! Go—

But as Kadijah tried to overtake the leader, she bumped into another skater who was trying to do the same thing.

Then another skater tripped over Kadijah and, like dominoes, all five skaters tumbled to the ground in a major wipeout.

A couple of the girls groaned in pain.

"Is everybody okay?" Kadijah asked as she struggled to sit up.

"We would've been if you hadn't bumped into me," Annie said.

"You made us trip!" Leesha said.

"This is so embarrassing," cried another.

Was Kadijah to blame? She wasn't sure, but either way, she felt awful. She'd ruined her chance.

A ref and a medic rushed over to the girls to make sure they were okay. Besides some scratches and bruised egos, they were all fine, thanks to their safety equipment.

The announcer's voice blared over the speaker system. "Due to a crash, this race is a scratch. However, no speed skater is disqualified. All skaters in heat six will have another chance next weekend to advance."

Kadijah slowly got to her feet, then helped another racer up. She gave a deep sigh as she skated slowly off the track.

My first real race, and I blew it, she thought.

CHAPTER 8

DOUBT

On Monday, Kadijah sat in math class. But math was the furthest thing from her mind. All she could think about was the wipeout that apparently she had caused.

"Kadijah? Kadijah Carrie?" the math teacher said. "Are you paying attention? What's the answer to number twelve?"

"Sorry, Mrs. Ramsey," Kadijah said, snapping out of her trance. She fumbled through her paper for the answer. "The answer is fifty-five, remainder two."

The teacher nodded, and Kadijah returned to her thoughts. She couldn't stop replaying the image of everyone, including herself, falling and crashing, ending her first race without even crossing the finish line.

At lunch, Kadijah, Zoey, and Damon sat together, as usual. But Kadijah was quiet as she poked at her cooked carrots.

"Hey KC, you're not eating your lunch at all," Zoey said.

Kadijah gently pushed her lunch tray toward her friends. "You can have it, guys. I'm not very hungry today."

"We don't want your food, KC. We're just really worried about you," Zoey said.

A boy named Zeke walked by their table with his phone blaring. "Hey guys, KC is all over ZooTube! Somebody posted her wreck at the race! Come look!"

Kadijah cowered over her tray and covered her head in shame.

"Come on, she doesn't want to see that! That's just mean! Turn it off!" snapped Damon.

"Hey, chill!" Zeke replied.

"Zeke, if that was you, I'm sure you wouldn't like people shoving a video in your face about it," Zoey said.

"Okay, okay. That was not cool of me. Sorry, KC," Zeke said, and held up his hands in apology.

Kadijah kept her head hidden. "It's okay," she mumbled.

Zeke gave a small shrug and walked away.

"Thanks for looking out for me, guys," Kadijah said as she lifted her head from the table.

"We're your friends. We've always got your back," Damon said.

"And if you want to talk about the race, or if you don't, we're here for you," Zoey chimed in. "We care about you, KC."

Kadijah tried to smile. "That means a lot. It's just that I got so cocky, and it cost me the race. And

I made all those other girls mad at me. Everyone saw it. Now it's on the internet too!"

"Well, next weekend you can get back out there and have a do-over," Damon said.

"I'm not so sure," Kadijah replied.

Zoey was confused. "What do you mean?"

Kadijah got up from the lunch table. "Guys, I don't feel so good. I'm going to the nurse. I'll see you later."

***

The following day, Kadijah lay in her room with a thermometer in her mouth. Moments later, her mom entered to check her temperature.

"You've been in bed since yesterday, but you don't have a fever or any other symptoms. You can't miss another day of class if you're not sick. And you missed practice with Trini yesterday," said Mom.

Kadijah let out a long sigh.

"Is this still about the race?" Mom asked. "Honey, it's going to be okay. We're proud of you. You shouldn't feel ashamed," Mom said.

Kadijah nodded as her phone buzzed. It was another text message from her friends. She'd been leaving them unread since coming home from school yesterday.

"Don't you want to talk to your friends? I bet they're really worried about you," said Mom.

Kadijah lifted her phone then quickly put it back down. "I can't. I'm just so embarrassed."

"Honey, everyone makes mistakes. It's not the end of the world. We learn from our mistakes so we can move forward, and this weekend you'll be able to move forward when you race again," Mom said.

"I don't know if I want to race again, Mom. I'm so scared to fail," Kadijah said.

"You can't stay in your room forever," Mom replied. "We love you and support you no matter what you choose to do. But tomorrow, it's back to school."

"Okay, Mom," Kadijah said with a sigh.

Mom gave Kadijah a kiss on the forehead and left the bedroom.

Kadijah threw the covers back over her head. But her phone buzzed again. And again. And again.

"UGH! Why doesn't everyone leave me alone!" yelled Kadijah, finally picking up her phone. She saw the latest text message from Zoey:

> we r outside yr house and not
> leaving til u come out. worried about
> u and want to make sure yr OK.
> Damon brought you ice cream—he
> said if u don't come outside in 5 min
> he's gonna eat it

Kadijah felt her lips pull into a small smile. *People do care about me,* she realized. She got out of bed, put on some shoes, and headed outside.

Zoey and Damon waved with both hands as they saw Kadijah approach. They had brought reinforcements—Trini and her friend Ivy were there too. They were all eating ice cream, and Damon handed Kadijah a quickly melting cone.

"Free ice cream can make anyone come outside. If you waited one more minute, you would have missed out," Damon joked.

"Thanks, guys," Kadijah said. "You didn't have to come check on me."

"You missed practice yesterday," Trini said. "When you didn't reply to my text, I texted Damon. He told me you were thinking about quitting. So we're here to talk you out of it."

Kadijah shook her head. "I'm just embarrassed. And scared. I made a fool of myself," she said. "I really don't know if I want to race again." She took a quick lick from her cone to catch the drips oozing down the sides.

"I get it," Trini said. "But part of sports—and

life—is about learning to get back up and trying again after you fall."

"Do you know how many times I've caused an accident in a race?" said Ivy. "I almost got kicked out of a racing league because of it! But, because I didn't give up and was surrounded by people who wanted to help me, I got better at speed skating and learned to avoid crashes. And I made a lot of cool friends!" She elbowed Trini and laughed.

"Really?" Kadijah said, surprised.

"We've all made mistakes, in a lot of things," said Damon. "Don't give up on yourself."

Trini put her hand on Kadijah's shoulder. "And it was only your first official race. If you quit now, all the hard work and effort that you've put into this will be for nothing. You can't end with a crash. You've got to get back out there and try again."

Kadijah looked at Trini and her friends. She smiled.

"Thanks for the pep talk," she said. "I'm tired

of beating myself up, and I really don't want to quit. I want to race this weekend, and no matter how I finish, I'll know that I didn't give up."

"Group hug!" shouted Zoey.

CHAPTER 9

LAST CHANCE TO QUALIFY

It was the weekend and round two of the Fairbright Speed Skating Tournament. Kadijah's parents had wished her luck and headed to the stands to watch the race. Kadijah was putting on her gear near the other racers in her heat. She was nervous about seeing them again.

Just then, Leesha walked over to Kadijah.

"Hey, I just wanted to say sorry for giving you so much attitude last week after we fell. I think we all were sort of to blame," she admitted.

Annie chimed in. "Yeah, I can't pretend like I've been a perfect racer my entire life, so I should apologize too."

"Thank you," Kadijah said. "That really means a lot to me. And this time, I promise not to knock everybody down!"

"Your friends told me that was your first ever race. My very first race, I hit the first turn so hard that I launched myself off the track!" Leesha said.

The girls all laughed and wished each other luck, then went back to getting ready.

Wow, that went better than I thought it would, Kadijah thought. *I can't believe I almost quit because I thought they'd all hate me . . .*

Kadijah's friends came over for a last-minute pep talk.

"Ready to race?" Trini asked.

"Ready!" Kadijah replied.

"Good. Remember, don't burn yourself out by going full blast in the first lap. Make sure to be on the outside of the other racers and not in the middle. You got this," said Trini.

Then she added, "By the way, my boss at The Burger Break was really impressed with your skills. She wanted me to tell you that if you want a summer job, you're hired."

"You mean I get to work with you, skate, *and* get paid? Awesome! Count me in!" said Kadijah. Her parents would be thrilled that she'd be earning some extra money.

The announcer's voice boomed over the loudspeaker. "The makeup race for the middle school girls heat six starts in five minutes. The top two racers advance to the state tournament. Proceed to the starting line!"

Kadijah's friends wished her luck as she skated over to the track.

The same five girls from the week before rolled up to join her.

This time, if we get caught up in a cluster, I'm going

to make sure to be on the outside and not in the middle.

"On your mark!" said the announcer.

The girls bent and leaned forward. Kadijah took a deep breath.

"Get set . . ."

Just do your best. Believe in yourself. You got this, Kadijah told herself.

Bang!

The skaters took off quickly. Kadijah found herself in last place right out of the gate. But as they got to the first turn, she was catching up to fourth place.

By the last turn of the first lap, Kadijah was side by side with the fourth place skater. She drafted for a moment to catch her breath.

Time to kick it into overdrive. NOW!

Kadijah zoomed ahead to take fourth place as they entered the second lap. Soon she was on third place's tail!

Okay, at the next turn make your move . . .

Kadijah went from drafting to passing and overtook third place.

Phew!

Now just two skaters were in her sights.

As they started the third lap, Kadijah was drafting behind the second place skater. She was gearing up to pass her, but the skaters behind them were starting to catch up too. Kadijah felt a moment of panic.

They're about to start crowding again! Do what Trini said—get on the outside of the group and don't get stuck in the cluster! But stay close to the second place skater . . .

Kadijah stopped drafting and quickly moved to the outside of the group to pull away from the cluster. It worked! Soon she was side by side with second place.

"Go, KC, go!" Zoey screamed.

"Go, Stealth Lightning!" yelled Damon.

"Final lap! You can do it, kiddo!" boomed Dad's voice.

The skaters were still huddled close to each other, going at full speed as they were about to start the fourth and final lap.

Kadijah was neck and neck with Leesha for second place. Annie was in first place, and Kadijah realized Annie was speeding up on the inside lane and taking an even bigger lead.

It's time to take control and see if I can draft my way toward the leader . . .

Kadijah turned it up a notch and took over second place. She kept at it to chase down Annie. By the third turn, she was drafting just inches behind her!

On the fourth turn, go all out. No matter what happens, just do your best.

As they approached the fourth turn, Kadijah worked to try to overtake Annie in the final stretch. She could feel Leesha and the others on her heels.

"Go, KC!" she heard from the stands.

But as fast as Kadijah was going, it wasn't fast

enough. Suddenly, she was in a race for second place as Leesha caught up to her again.

Annie crossed the finish line, with Kadijah and Leesha crossing the line together a second later.

Kadijah panted as she rolled to a stop. The crowd was going wild. She couldn't believe it. She hadn't given up. She had shown up and she had raced, even when it got hard. She hadn't won, but she couldn't contain her smile.

"It looks like we've got a photo finish for second!" called the announcer. "We'll have the results shortly."

No matter what happens, it's okay. I'm here, and that's a win, Kadijah thought.

The skaters were still panting and shaking hands when Kadijah's parents and friends rushed over.

"You didn't give up on yourself and look what happened. You had a great race!" said Trini.

Kadijah nodded and gave her a big hug.

"Awesome job, KC!" said Damon.

"We're so proud of you, kiddo," said Dad. "You gave it all you could."

"Hey, the announcer has the results! Listen!" said Zoey.

The announcer cleared his throat. "It looks like *three* skaters will be advancing to the state tournament, as there's a tie for second! Congratulations to our winners—Annie Johnson in first place, and Kadijah Carrie and Leesha Roberts tied for second!"

Kadijah screamed. "I did it! I did it! I can't believe I'm going to the state tournament!"

She looked at her friends and family and then turned to Trini.

"Thank you for being such a great coach and for believing in me," Kadijah said. "You gave me the push to get back out here and prove myself. I couldn't have done any of this without you!"

"Coaching you is fun," Trini said. "But it's not over yet. You've got a state tournament to prepare for, KC!"

"See you at practice on Monday, coach?" asked Kadijah.

"See you Monday, KC," Trini replied.

GLOSSARY

advantage (ad-VAN-tej)—a benefit or upper hand over others

agile (AJ-ile)—able to move gracefully and easily

attitude (ATT-uh-tood)—actions or words that can affect oneself and others

cocky (COCK-ee)—confidence that may be off-putting to others

coincidence (co-IN-sih-dinss)—when events happen by chance at the same time that seem related or connected

draft (DRAFT)—to skate behind another to reduce air friction

ego (EE-go)—a sense of oneself

exert (eg-ZURT)—to try or give effort

fixate (FIX-ayt)—to be very focused on something

humiliation (hew-mill-ee-AY-shun)—extreme embarrassment

impending (im-PENN-ding)—going to happen

interval (IN-terr-vuhl)—a type of training that alternates between a fast pace and a period of rest

league (LEEG)—group or organization for a sport

momentum (mo-MEN-tum)—strength or force gained by motion

mopey (MOH-pee)—acting sulky or disappointed

obstacle (OBB-stuh-kul)—something in the way

panic (PAN-uk)—sudden feeling of worry

posture (PAWST-chur)—the position of the body

promotion (pro-MOH-shun)—a raise or higher position

sensation (sen-SAY-shun)—a feeling

spandex (SPAN-dex)—a stretchy material

stamina (STAM-ih-huh)—ability to maintain prolonged effort

stealth (STELTH)—secret, quiet, or surprising

trance (TRANSS)—a state of being unaware of things around you

trial (TRY-uhl)—a preliminary race

DISCUSSION QUESTIONS

1. Have you ever been roller skating or skateboarding before? If you have, how would you describe the feeling of standing on wheels for the very first time?

2. In this story, we discover that this is the first time Kadijah has stuck with an organized sport. She felt a lot of pressure to succeed. Have you ever had a fear of failing while playing a sport? How did you overcome it?

3. Trini serves as a trainer and mentor for Kadijah. A mentor is usually an older person who looks out for you, gives advice, and tries to help. Do you have any mentors in your life? Are you a mentor to a younger person?

WRITING PROMPTS

1. Zoey and Damon are good and supportive friends to Kadijah. Make a list of the things they do in the story that show their support. Now imagine that Kadijah has an opportunity to return the favor. How might she support her friends when they are facing a challenge?

2. It can be interesting to think about a story from a different point of view. Try writing the final chapter from Kadijah's parents' point of view. What was going through their minds as they watched the race?

3. Kadijah spent weeks training and exercising with Trini to prepare for the Speed Skating Tournament. What kind of exercises would you do to prepare for it? Write up a training plan for this event, or another sporting event you might be preparing for.

MORE ABOUT INLINE SPEED SKATING

- The inventor of the inline roller skate is thought to be John Joseph Merlin from Belgium. In the 1760s, this inventor and instrument maker wore the skates he made as a way to promote his museum. However, Merlin's skates had no brakes, which caused lots of problems.

- In 1910, a three-wheeled inline skate was created for roller hockey players in New York. The skates were designed by the Roller Hockey Skate Company.

- In 1937, the first Roller Speed Skating World Championship was held in Monza, Italy.

- In 1979, brothers Scott and Brennan Olson from Minneapolis modified a pair of older inline skates. They attached four-wheeled inline skate frames to a pair of hockey boots. They also installed a rubber toe-brake so the skater could stop more easily. Their skates were meant for ice hockey training during the off-season, but their idea took off and became known as Rollerblades—the modern inline skates many use today.

- Inline roller speed skating, also called inline racing, has been a part of the World Games since 1981.

- During the 1992 Summer Olympic Games in Barcelona, Spain, inline skate rink hockey, using quad skates, was performed as a demonstration sport. It was the first time that roller skating athletes were part of the Olympics.

- By 1997, inline skating had become a billion-dollar business, with more than 25 million Americans participating in it.

- In 2021, at the Inline Speed Skating World Championships, the nation of Colombia won 59 out of a possible 126 medals. The United States won just one bronze medal overall.

- Today there are a number of competitive inline skating sports. In addition to inline speed skating, there's inline alpine, inline downhill, inline freestyle, and inline hockey.

- Inline speed skating and ice speed skating are similar enough that some athletes compete in both sports. Five years after switching from inline speed skating to ice speed skating, U.S. skater Erin Jackson was the top-ranked ice speed skater in the world at the 500-meter event. She won gold in the 2022 Beijing Olympics.

- Have you ever wondered how fast it's possible to go on inline speed skates? The average speed of an inline speed skater is anywhere from 6 to 20 miles (9.7 to 32.2 kilometers) per hour. Elite athletes may reach up to 31 mph (50 kph). Skaters can go as fast as 40 mph (64.4 kph) while skating downhill!

- Some people use inline skating as a form of exercise. Skating at a speed of 8 to 9 mph (13 to 14 kph) can burn more than 300 calories an hour.

- Aggressive inline skating (also known as rollerblading, blading, skating, street skating, rolling, roller freestyle, or freestyle rolling) is a type of inline skating in the "extreme sports" category. Aggressive inline skates are modified to be able to do grinds and jumps similar to skateboards.

- Roller speed skating races are held on rinks with banked walls or on closed roads. A maximum of five wheels are allowed on racers' skates, and cannot be bigger than 110mm. For long distances, skates can have 125mm wheels. In professional events, no brakes are allowed!

To learn more about inline speed skating, check out these websites:

olympics.com/en/sports/roller-speed-skating/

teamusa.org/usa-roller-sports/speed-skating

worldskate.org/news/17-world-skate/2408-roller-speed-skating-conquers-the-olympics-the-first-medals-at-the-yog-buenos-aires-2018.html

jumponwheels.com/how-fast-can-inline-speed-skates-go/

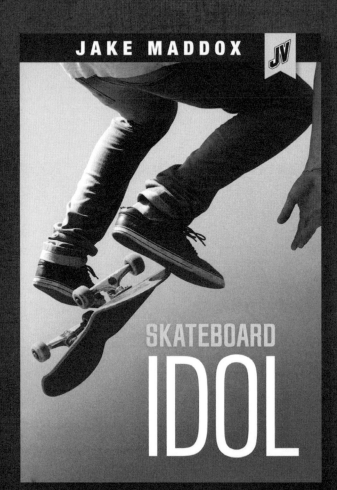

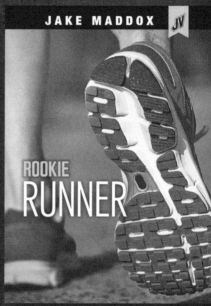

ABOUT the AUTHOR

SHAWN PRYOR's (he/him) work includes the middle-grade graphic novel series Cash and Carrie, *The Deadliest Race* from the Scary Graphics series, several books for Capstone's Jake Maddox Sports and Adventure series, and the Kids Sports series.

In his free time, Shawn enjoys reading, cooking, listening to music, and talking about why Zack from the *Mighty Morphin Power Rangers* is the greatest superhero of all time.